THE SECRET OF THE HIDDEN SCROLLS

BOOK SEVEN
THE KING IS BORN

BY M. J. THOMAS

WORTHY
kids™

For my son, Peter. Thank you for your creative idea,
encouragement, and help with the books!

—M.J.T.

ISBN: 978-1-5460-1463-8

WorthyKids
Hachette Book Group
1290 Avenue of the Americas
New York, NY 10104

LCCN: 2019944106

Cover illustration by Graham Howells
Interior illustrations by Lisa S. Reed
Designed by Georgina Chidlow-Irvin

Lexile® level 460L

Printed and bound in the U.S.A.
CW
10 9 8 7

CONTENTS

PROLOGUE

Nine-year-old Peter and his ten-year-old sister, Mary, stood at the door to the huge, old house and waved as their parents drove away. Peter and Mary and their dog, Hank, would be spending the month with Great-Uncle Solomon.

Peter thought it would be the most boring month ever—until he realized Great-Uncle Solomon was an archaeologist. Great-Uncle Solomon showed them artifacts and treasures and told them stories about his travels around the globe. And then he shared his most amazing discovery of all—the Legend of the Hidden Scrolls! These weren't just dusty old scrolls. They held secrets—and they would lead to travel through time.

Soon Peter, Mary, and Hank were flung back in time to important moments in the Bible. They witnessed the Creation of the earth. They helped Noah load the ark before the flood. They endured the plagues in Egypt. They watched as David battled Goliath, and they faced lions with Daniel. They had exciting adventures, all while trying to solve the secrets in the scrolls.

Now Peter and Mary are ready for their next adventure . . . as soon as they hear the lion's roar.

The Legend of the Hidden Scrolls

THE SCROLLS CONTAIN THE TRUTH YOU SEEK.

BREAK THE SEAL. UNROLL THE SCROLL.

AND YOU WILL SEE THE PAST UNFOLD.

AMAZING ADVENTURES ARE IN STORE

FOR THOSE WHO FOLLOW THE LION'S ROAR!

1

AN EARLY CHRISTMAS

"Where's the star?" shouted Peter from the top of the ladder.

Mary dug through a box full of Christmas decorations. "I don't see it."

Great-Uncle Solomon looked around the living room. "I think it's in that pile of ornaments next to the fireplace."

"Hank, find the star," said Peter.

Hank ran over to the ornaments and started pawing through the pile.

"*Woof!*" Hank barked, then grabbed the star

and ran toward the tall Christmas tree.

"Stop!" shouted Peter.

It was too late. Hank jumped straight for the top of the Christmas tree.

"Stop him!" shouted Mary.

Peter jumped from the ladder and caught Hank in midair just before he crashed into the tree. Hank and Peter tumbled across the floor.

Great-Uncle Solomon let out a deep breath. "That was close!"

Hank stood up with the star still in his mouth and wagged his tail.

"Good boy, Hank," said Peter. "You found the star!"

Mary scowled and put her hands on her hips.

"He did. But he almost knocked over the whole tree too!"

Peter took the star from Hank and climbed the ladder. "He was just trying to help," said Peter. He placed the star on top of the tree.

Great-Uncle Solomon adjusted his round glasses and looked up at the star. "It's perfect!"

"Thank you," said Peter as he climbed down.

Mary placed a few more ornaments on the tree. "It does look nice," she said. "But I'm a little confused."

"Really? That's strange," said Peter. Mary was never confused.

Great-Uncle Solomon hung the last ornament on the tree. "What are you confused about?"

"It's the middle of summer," said Mary. "Why are we putting up a Christmas tree?"

"Well, I've never been able to spend Christmas with you two," said Great-Uncle Solomon. "So

I wanted to celebrate before your parents come back from their trip and take you home."

Peter thought about his parents. It had been almost three weeks since they had dropped off Peter and Mary at Great-Uncle Solomon's house and traveled to Africa to build a school. "I really miss them."

Mary's shoulders slumped. "Me too. I wish they could be here with us."

Great-Uncle Solomon put his arm around Mary's shoulders. "They'll be with you soon enough," he said. "Until then, I have gifts for you!"

Peter perked up. He loved gifts.

"But it's not Christmas yet," said Mary.

Peter gave Mary a look. "Come on, Mary, get in the Christmas spirit."

"I think you'll like them," said Great-Uncle Solomon. "And they might be helpful on your next adventure."

Mary's eyebrows shot up. Peter could tell she wanted to know what the gifts were.

"I'll be right back," said Great-Uncle Solomon. He dashed out of the room.

Great-Uncle Solomon came back into the room carrying three packages wrapped in newspaper. He sat down on the couch and handed the first package to Mary.

She ripped the paper off and opened the box. Peter looked over her shoulder.

"What is it?" asked Mary.

"It's a map," said Peter.

"I know it's a map," said Mary. "A map of what—I mean where?"

"It's a map of ancient Israel," said Great-Uncle Solomon. "But it's not just any map—it's very special!"

Mary's eyes got as big as globes. "What's special about it?"

"I was on an archaeology dig near Babylon when I found the remains of an ancient library," said Great-Uncle Solomon. "There were many scrolls with stories of travel and adventure. I also found maps of star constellations and ancient lands."

"What about Mary's map?" asked Peter.

"Oh, yes. I was just getting to that," said Great-Uncle Solomon. "May I see the map, Mary?"

"Sure," said Mary, handing it over.

As Great-Uncle Solomon unrolled the dusty, old map, Peter noticed that the top right corner was missing.

"Hidden in the maps of the constellations, I found this map of ancient Israel," Great-Uncle Solomon said. "I came to believe that it's more than two thousand years old and might have been used by the Magi as they followed God's special star to search for the newborn King."

"What are Magi?" asked Peter.

"The Magi were wise men from the Middle East who studied the stars," said Mary. "They were respected by kings and people everywhere for their knowledge and wisdom."

"You are correct," said Great-Uncle Solomon. "You know a lot about history!"

Peter shook his head. Of course, Mary was right—she was always right.

"Thank you," said Mary. "For the gift and the compliment."

Peter opened his gift next. He ripped off the paper and tore open the box. Inside, he found a bronze telescope.

"I discovered this telescope on a dig in Italy," said Great-Uncle Solomon. "It is one of the first telescopes ever made."

"Who made it?" asked Mary.

"It was made by Galileo in the early 1600s," answered Great-Uncle Solomon.

Peter laughed. "Then it's almost as old as you."

Great-Uncle Solomon chuckled. "Almost," he said, handing the last gift to Hank. "Here you go, Hank."

Newspaper flew everywhere as Hank ripped into the package and found a long bone. He plopped down on the floor and started chewing on it.

"Is that an old dinosaur bone?" asked Peter.

"Oh no," said Great-Uncle Solomon. He tapped his chin. "Well, at least I don't think it is."

Roar!

The lion's roar echoed loudly through the house. It was so loud it made the ornaments on the Christmas tree shake.

"It's time for your next adventure!" said Great-Uncle Solomon. "Take your gifts!"

"Let's go!" said Peter.

Peter, Mary, and Hank ran out of the living room, past the shiny suit of armor, and down the long hallway to the library.

Peter ran across the hallway and grabbed his adventure bag. "I don't want to forget this." He put his telescope inside, and Mary put her map on top.

Hank held up his bone and wagged his tail.

"Okay," said Peter. "We can take your bone."

He grabbed the slobbery bone and put it in the bag.

Roar! The lion's roar came from behind the tall, wooden library doors that reminded Peter of a castle.

"Hurry and open it!" said Mary.

Peter reached for the handle shaped like a lion's head.

Click. Peter turned the handle and opened the door.

Roar! The sound came from behind the tall bookshelf on the right.

Hank ran to the bookshelf and barked.

Mary pulled a book from the shelf. It was red with a lion's head painted in gold on the cover.

The bookshelf rumbled and slid open to reveal a hidden room. It was dark except for a glowing clay pot filled with ancient scrolls in the center of the room.

Peter, Mary, and Hank circled the glowing pot and looked at the scrolls.

"Which one should we pick this time?" asked Mary.

Hank sniffed one of the scrolls and barked.

"What's on the seal of that one?" asked Peter.

Mary picked up the scroll and looked at the red wax seal. "It's a star."

"Hank sure is good at finding stars," said Peter. "Let's see where the star takes us!"

Mary broke the red wax seal. Suddenly, the walls shook, books fell off the shelves, and the floor quaked. The library crumbled around them and disappeared. Then everything was still and quiet.

2

A Slippery Slope

Peter tucked the scroll into his bag and looked down at dry, rocky ground. Grass and shrubs speckled the hilltop where he and Mary stood.

Mary looked around. "Where are we?"

Peter walked to the edge of the hill and looked down the rocky slope. "I think we're in the middle of nowhere."

"We have to be *somewhere*," said Mary.

"You're probably right," said Peter.

"Where's the map Great-Uncle Solomon gave me?" asked Mary.

Peter dug in the bag and handed the old map to Mary. Then he pulled out his telescope and looked into the distance.

"Do you see any landmarks?" asked Mary.

"All I see is rocks and sand," said Peter. "It looks like a desert."

"Look farther," said Mary.

Peter pulled out the lens of the telescope, making it longer. "Wow! You can really see a long way with this thing."

Mary tapped her foot. "What do you see?"

"Oh yeah!" said Peter. "I see water. It looks like a huge lake."

Mary pointed at the map. "Like this?"

Peter lowered the telescope and looked at the map. Then he looked back through the telescope. "Yes!" he said. "That's it!"

"It's the Dead Sea," said Mary.

"It doesn't look dead to me," said Peter.

Mary rolled her eyes. "It's not *dead* dead," she said. "It's called the Dead Sea because it's the lowest place on earth and has so much salt that no fish can live in it."

"How do you know so much about it?" said Peter.

"I read about it in a book called *My Life by the Dead Sea*."

Peter shook his head. "Sounds boring."

"It was a *deep* book," said Mary.

Peter laughed. "That's funny."

"You're not the only funny one in the family," said Mary. "Now let's go see what's on the other side of the hill."

They walked across the hilltop, and Peter looked through the telescope again.

"I see a big city on a hill," said Peter. "It has a lot of stone buildings. There's a palace and towers and . . . oh wow!"

"What?" said Mary.

"A really big white building with tall columns and a gold roof!"

Mary studied the map. "That must be Jerusalem."

"It looks cool," said Peter. "Let's go there!"

"Woof!" Hank barked and trotted ahead.

"I don't know," said Mary. "It seems really far away on the map."

Peter held up the telescope and looked through it. Then he looked at the sun beginning to set in the distance.

"Yeah, it's pretty far. I don't think we can make it before dark."

"Do you see anything closer?" asked Mary.

Peter scanned the horizon with the telescope. "I see a little town with some small buildings and houses," said Peter. "It's between us and Jerusalem."

Mary ran her finger along the map. "It's Bethlehem!"

"We've been there!" said Peter. "That's where King David grew up."

"Maybe we can find a place to sleep there," said Mary.

Peter's stomach growled. "And maybe we can find some food."

"Let's hurry before it gets dark!" said Mary.

Peter put the map and telescope back in the adventure bag. He headed down the rocky slope with Mary trailing behind. The climb was challenging, and Peter's legs started to ache. Hank easily hopped from rock to rock.

"Wait for us!" shouted Peter.

"Ruff!" Hank came to a stop at the bottom of the hill.

"We're almost there," said Peter. He turned and saw Mary a few feet behind him. He took another step and slipped on gravel. He fell and slid to the bottom of the hill.

"Ouch!" Peter heard laughter behind him. "It's not funny, Mary!"

"That wasn't me," said Mary.

Peter froze. "Then who was it?"

Mary pointed at an opening in the side of the hill. "It came from in there."

Laughter echoed out of the cave.

Mary bolted down the side of the hill and slid to a stop beside Peter and Hank.

"I didn't know you could move that fast!" said Peter.

Mary took deep breaths. "Neither did I!"

Peter looked up at the cave as three large animals stepped out. They had sharp fangs and their eyes darted from side to side.

"Hyenas," whispered Mary.

"I hope they're not as hungry as I am," said Peter.

3

No Room in the Inn

"Grrrr!" Hank stood in front of Peter and Mary and growled at the hyenas running down the hill.

Peter's heart pounded as the hyenas slowly circled around them.

"Woof! Woof!" Hank barked and paced between the hyenas and Peter and Mary.

The hyenas growled and laughed and snapped at Hank.

"They may be laughing," said Peter. "But they don't look too happy."

"What do we do?" said Mary. "I don't think my karate will help."

Peter reached into the adventure bag. "I have an idea!"

"I don't think a map is going to help either," said Mary.

Peter pulled out Hank's bone. "Hey, hyenas, want a bone?" He waved it in the air.

The hyenas' ears perked up. They stopped pacing and stared at Peter.

"Stay, Hank!" said Peter. Then he threw the bone as far up the hill as he could. It soared through the air, and the hyenas raced after it. Peter and Mary watched as the hyenas started fighting over the bone.

"That should keep them busy for a while," said Peter.

"We need to run while they're distracted!" said Mary.

They ran across
the stony terrain
and stopped at a
small dirt road.

Peter looked
up. The sun was
almost gone and
the sky had grown
darker.

"Let's hurry and
get to Bethlehem
before it gets too
dark," said Mary.

"And before
those hyenas finish that bone," said Peter.

They walked down the winding, dusty road.
They moved a little slower with every step.

"Bethlehem is farther away than it looked
from the hill," said Peter.

Mary sat down on a rock. "I'm so tired," she said. "I don't think I can keep going."

Peter pointed at the little town in front of them. "Come on, Mary," he said. "We're almost there. You can do it!"

"Okay," said Mary. "I'll try."

Peter took Mary's hand and helped her up.

The air got colder after the sun set. And soon, they made it to Bethlehem.

"It looks different than when we were here before," said Mary.

"Yeah," said Peter. "There are more buildings and it's a lot busier."

People bumped and pushed, and donkeys crossed in front of them.

"Let's try to find some place to sleep," said Mary. "I don't think I can walk another step."

Peter saw people going in and out of a small building. There were several donkeys tied to a post outside. "Let's go over there," he said.

They walked up the stone path and entered the front door.

A large man sat on a pillow behind a table counting money. "Welcome to The King David Inn," he mumbled.

"He doesn't sound very friendly," whispered Peter.

"What do you want?" grunted the innkeeper.

"We want a place to sleep," said Peter.

Mary shivered. "We've come a long way and we are very tired."

"And hungry," said Peter.

The man picked up a piece of bread and took a big bite. "No," he said. Crumbs fell from his mouth as he spoke. "I don't have any room in the inn. No one has any rooms."

"Where are we supposed to go?" asked Mary.

"I don't know," said the innkeeper. "But you can't stay here."

He pointed to the door. "Now get out of here!"

"*Grrrr.*" Hank growled.

"Leave!" shouted the innkeeper. "And keep that dog away from me!"

Peter, Mary, and Hank rushed out into the crowded street.

Peter saw a large sign nailed to a post beside the inn. It was written in a strange language Peter didn't recognize. "What do you think it says?"

Mary looked at the sign. "It's written in Latin," she said.

"Can you read Latin?" said Peter.

"I hope so," said Mary. "I've studied Latin for three years."

"Well, what does it say?"

Mary studied the sign and read slowly. *"A Decree of Caesar Augustus—All people must travel to their hometown and be registered."*

"I guess that's why Bethlehem is so crowded," said Peter. "Everyone is traveling."

"Woof! Woof!" Hank ran behind the inn.

Mary and Peter ran after him. They rounded the corner and saw a small stable with donkeys and sheep. Hank was lying on a pile of hay.

Mary said, "Yuck! What's that smell?"

"Probably the animals," said Peter. "But I'm so tired, I don't even care."

Mary spread out some hay on the ground.

Peter set the adventure bag down near the entrance of the stable. Then he nestled down on the bed of hay and drifted off to sleep.

Peter woke to the sound of a rooster crowing. He shook Mary's shoulder to wake her.

"*Grrrr.*" Hank stood at the front of the stable.

"What is it, Hank?" said Peter.

The innkeeper stepped into the stable. "I told you kids to leave!" he said.

"We're very sorry," said Mary. "We were cold and tired and had nowhere else to go."

"Well, now you must pay for staying in my inn," said the innkeeper.

"But we don't have any money," said Peter.

The innkeeper spotted the adventure bag. He reached down and grabbed it. "This looks nice," he said. "I will take it as payment."

4

LOST IN THE CROWD

Peter looked at the innkeeper. Then he looked at the bag tucked under his arm.

"No! Please don't take it," said Peter. "It's all we have."

"Then maybe I will take your dog," said the innkeeper. He walked toward Hank.

"*Grrrr.*" Hank growled as the innkeeper walked toward him.

"Or maybe not," said the innkeeper.

"I'll work for you," said Peter. "But please give me the bag."

"No," said the innkeeper. He smiled. "I'm keeping it."

"You shouldn't pick on kids," muttered Peter.

"And who's going to stop me?" asked the innkeeper.

Peter gave Mary the thumbs-up. "You're about to find out."

Mary ran across the stable and did a spinning kick that hit the innkeeper right in the arm. The leather bag flew into the air. The innkeeper fell back into a pile of hay.

"Get the bag, Hank!" shouted Peter.

Hank jumped and caught the bag just before it

hit the floor. He trotted over and dropped it at Peter's feet.

"Good boy, Hank," said Peter.

"Let's get out of here," said Mary.

Peter, Mary, and Hank raced out of the stable and hurried down the busy street.

Peter looked back. "I think we're safe now."

"That was close," said Mary.

Ahead, Peter saw everyone heading in the same direction. "I wonder where they're going?"

"Let's find out," said Mary.

They followed the crowd down the dusty street. Everyone Peter saw looked sad or tired.

"Grrrr!" Peter heard Hank growl behind him.

Peter quickly turned around and saw a soldier riding a tall white horse. The soldier wore a red cape and shiny, silver armor. His helmet had a bright red plume sticking out of the top, and a sword hung by his side.

"Everyone line up to be registered!" shouted the soldier.

The people slowly lined up at a wooden table piled with scrolls. More soldiers sat behind the table.

Peter tapped the man in front of them on the shoulder. "What's everyone registering for?"

The man looked at him and frowned. "We have to register with the Roman Empire so they can make us pay taxes."

"Hurry up!" said the soldier from his horse. "Let's make this fast so I can get out of this boring little town!"

"He sure is in a bad mood," said Mary.

"The Commander is always in a bad mood," said the man. "He acts like he rules Israel."

"Does he?" asked Peter.

"Not officially," said the man. "But everyone does what he says."

"Silence!" roared the Commander. "Stay in line and do as you're told!"

The man quickly turned around and got back in line.

"Let's get out of here," whispered Mary.

They turned and walked away from the line. Peter heard hooves galloping up behind him.

"Stop right there!" said a stern voice.

Peter, Mary, and Hank froze in their tracks.

"Where do you think you're going?" the voice asked.

Peter slowly turned and saw the Commander looking down at them from his horse. Peter shielded his eyes from the sun reflecting off the Commander's armor.

"We were just leaving," said Peter.

"You're not going anywhere until you register," said the Commander.

"But we're not from Bethlehem," said Mary.

The Commander climbed down from his horse. He wrinkled his brow and looked at Peter and Mary's clothes. "Well, you certainly don't look like you're from Bethlehem."

"We're traveling," said Peter.

"Traveling from where?" the Commander asked.

"It's hard to explain," said Mary.

"Well, try," growled the Commander.

Peter's heart pounded. His mind raced for something to say.

"Commander!" shouted one of the soldiers. "We have a problem."

"Wait here," said the Commander. "I'll be right back!" He drew his sword and walked toward the registration desk.

"Let's get out of here!" said Peter. "We can't tell him we're from the future."

Mary looked nervously over her shoulder. "That's true, but where are we going to go?"

"I don't know," said Peter. "But we can't stay here."

Mary took a deep breath. "Okay, let's go."

Peter, Mary, and Hank dashed and darted through the crowd and kept going until they reached the edge of Bethlehem. As they ran out of the city gate, Peter bumped into a donkey. He looked up. A young lady was riding the donkey, and a young man was leading it.

"I'm sorry," said Peter.

"It's okay," said the lady. She gave Peter a kind smile.

Peter watched as the young couple walked past him toward Bethlehem.

"Just a little longer," said the man. "Our long journey is almost over. We have finally reached Bethlehem."

The woman wrapped her arms around her very round belly. "Hurry!" she said. "It's almost time."

5

THE BIG, BIG NEWS

Peter watched as the strangers entered Bethlehem.

He turned to Mary and Hank. "I hope they have a better time finding a place to stay than we did," said Peter.

They walked along the dusty road for a few minutes.

Peter turned and looked back toward Bethlehem. "I don't see the Commander," he said. "I think we're safe."

"Now what?" said Mary.

Peter reached in the bag, pulled out the map,

and handed it to Mary. "See where the closest town is," said Peter. He felt his stomach rumble. "I'm really hungry."

Mary sat down on a rock and looked at the map. "It looks like Jerusalem is the closest place."

Peter rubbed his stomach. "That's pretty far away."

All of a sudden, Peter heard whistling coming from the top of a nearby hill.

Hanks ears perked up. He took off running up the hill.

"Wait!" shouted Peter.

Peter chased Hank up the hill, with Mary right behind him. When Peter reached the hilltop, he saw Hank racing around several sheep. Hank ran in a big circle, and the sheep came together in the middle of the hill.

Peter saw a boy carrying a shepherd's staff.

The boy bent over to pet Hank. "Good dog!"

"Hank, come!" shouted Peter.

Hank ran over and stood beside Peter.

"I'm sorry our dog scared your sheep," said Mary.

"Don't be sorry," said the boy. "Your dog helped! I've been chasing sheep around all day."

The boy lowered his head, "I'm not a very good shepherd," he said. "The sheep won't listen to me."

"I'm glad our dog could help," said Peter.

"Thank you," said the boy. "My name is Luke." He shook Peter's hand.

"I'm Peter and this is Hank," said Peter.

Hank put his paw up to shake Luke's hand.

Luke shook Hank's paw. "What an amazing dog you have!"

"Thanks," said Peter. "I trained him."

Mary tapped Peter on the shoulder.

"Oh yeah," he said. "This is my sister, Mary."

Luke smiled. "It's nice to meet you."

"It's nice to meet you too," Mary said.

Luke looked at their clothes. "You don't look like you're from around here."

"We're not," said Mary. "We're on a long journey."

"Where are you going?" asked Luke.

"We went to Bethlehem," said Peter. "But there was nowhere to sleep."

"Now we're going to Jerusalem to see if we can find a place there," said Mary.

Luke leaned against his staff. "That's pretty far," he said. "I don't know if you can make it before dark."

"Do you know a closer place?" said Mary.

Peter's stomach growled. "That has food?"

"I know the perfect place," said the shepherd boy. "And there's lots of food."

"Sounds good to me," said Peter.

"Follow me!" said Luke. He led them down the back side of the hill.

"Woof! Woof!" Hank barked and ran around the sheep. He kept them together and made them follow right behind Luke.

Peter started to sweat as they climbed one hill—then another.

"Where are we going?" asked Mary.

Peter turned in a circle. "Yeah, I don't see any houses."

"I don't live in a house," said Luke. "I live in the fields with the sheep."

"I guess that will work," said Peter. "As long as I get something to eat."

41

Luke smiled. "It's just over this hill."

When they reached the top of the hill, Peter looked down on a beautiful, grassy valley. A little creek ran along the bottom of the valley, weaving between trees. Sheep and shepherds were everywhere. Peter heard *baas* as the shepherds called to their sheep.

"This is perfect!" said Mary.

Hank ran down the hill. He circled the sheep and brought them down into the valley and into a pen with Luke.

Luke came back with olives and cheese and bread to eat. They sat in the grass and ate until they couldn't eat another bite. The sun began to set behind the distant hills.

"Follow me," said Luke. "I know the perfect place for you to sleep."

He took them to an olive tree on top of a hill.

"I'll see you in the morning," said Luke. Peter

watched him walk down the hill and join the other shepherds.

Hank curled up under the olive tree.

Peter looked into the night sky. He reached into his bag and pulled out his telescope. "Look at all those beautiful stars!"

Mary came up beside him. "Let me see."

"Wow!" said Peter. "There is a huge, bright star right over Bethlehem."

Mary tapped Peter on the shoulder. "Let me have a turn."

"There's another big one!" said Peter. "And it's coming right toward us!"

"Woof! Woof!"

"That's not a star!" said Mary. "It's Michael!"

Peter put down his telescope as Michael the angel landed beside them. He had a big grin on his face.

"I have some *BIG* news for you!" he said.

"What is it?" said Mary.

"Be patient," Michael said. "First, I have to give you the rules of your adventure."

"Can't you tell us the news first?" asked Peter.

"Not yet," said Michael. He held up one finger. "First rule: you have to solve the secret of the scroll in seven days or you will be stuck here."

Mary reached in the adventure bag and pulled out the scroll. She unrolled it. "The scroll has four words on it."

Peter looked over her shoulder. "What language is that?"

"It looks like Aramaic," said Mary.

"Can you read it?" said Peter. Mary always knew everything.

"No," said Mary. "I only learned the Aramaic alphabet. I don't know any words."

Peter shook his head. "You really need to study more."

Michael held up two fingers. "Second rule: you can't tell anyone where you are from or that you came from the future."

Peter and Mary nodded their heads.

Michael held up three fingers. "Third rule: you can't try to change the past."

"We won't," said Peter. "Now what is the *BIG* news?"

"Everything is about to change!" said Michael. "The time has come!"

"Time for what?" asked Mary.

"God's plan to rescue his people is starting right now!" said Michael.

"That *is* big news!" said Peter.

"God has been preparing for this day for a long, long time," said Michael.

"What's going to happen?" said Peter.

Michael pointed to the sky. "God is sending the Messiah and King to be with his people, just like he promised!"

"God loves his people so much that he is sending his only Son to save them," said Michael.

"What is he saving them from?" asked Peter.

"Remember how Adam and Eve disobeyed God and sin entered the world?" said Michael.

"Yes," said Mary. "Everything got worse."

"Sin separates people from God," Michael said. "And Satan wants to keep people separated from God so that he can rule this world. But God won't let that happen. He has a plan to rescue his people!"

"So Satan doesn't want this to happen?" asked Peter.

"No, he will do anything he can to stop God's plan," said Michael. "But remember that God is more powerful than the enemy."

"We'll remember," said Mary.

"And remember to be on the lookout for Satan," said Michael. "Make sure he doesn't find the new King!"

"We will," said Peter.

Michael looked up. "I have to go!" He spread his mighty wings and flew off into the starry night sky.

Then everything went dark—completely dark.

6

An Explosion of Light

Peter stared into the darkness. Then an explosion of light filled the night sky and flooded the valley below. An angel appeared, and Peter gasped.

He looked down from the hill and saw sheep scattering and the shepherds hiding behind trees.

"Do not be afraid!" the angel said to the shepherds. "I bring good news that will bring joy to the world. Today, in the city of David, the Savior is born, Christ the Lord. Here is a sign: you will find the baby wrapped in cloth and lying in a manger."

The shepherds gathered together and stared into the sky.

Peter looked around. The sky was filled with angels as far as he could see. They started to sing, and Peter thought it was the most beautiful sound he had ever heard.

"Glory to God in the highest and peace to all people on earth," sang the angels.

Peter noticed a familiar face in the angel choir. "Look," he said to Mary. "It's Michael!"

Michael smiled and waved.

The angels finished their song and disappeared into the night sky. Peter blinked in the sudden darkness.

"Michael was right," said Peter. "That was *BIG* news!"

Peter pulled out his telescope. He couldn't see any angels. They were gone. He turned his telescope to Bethlehem.

"Can you see anything?" asked Mary.

"No angels," said Peter. "But that one bright star is still over Bethlehem. It's shining down into the town."

"*Woof!*" Hank barked as someone came over the top of the hill.

Peter quickly put the telescope in his bag.

"Luke!" said Peter.

"Did you see that?" said Luke.

"Yes!" said Mary. "It was amazing!"

"I talked to the other shepherds," said Luke.

"We're going to go find the baby the angels told us about. Come with us!"

"Where do we go?" asked Peter.

"The angel said the baby was born in the city of David. That's another name for Bethlehem," said Luke. "So the baby must be in Bethlehem."

"The angel gave us another clue," said Mary.

"What?" asked Luke.

"He said we would find the baby in a manger," she said.

"You're right!" said Luke. "But why would a

baby be in an animals' feeding trough? Mangers can be nasty."

"Maybe there was nowhere else to go," said Mary. "We had to stay in a stable last night."

Peter snapped his fingers. "I think I know where the manger is!"

"Really? Where?" asked Luke.

"Hey, Mary," said Peter, "do you remember seeing a manger in the stable we slept in behind The King David Inn?"

"I do!" said Mary. "But how do we know that's *the* manger the angels were talking about?"

Peter thought for a minute. "I guess we don't. But we can check it out."

"Let's get the other shepherds," said Luke. "They'll want to go too."

Peter, Mary, and Hank followed Luke and the shepherds as they headed through the dark night to Bethlehem. They walked quietly through the city's gate and headed down the dusty street to the center of town.

Mary pointed. "There's The King David Inn!"

"The stable is around the corner," said Peter.

The shepherds walked up the stone path toward the front door.

"Wait!" Peter whispered. "Don't go in there. Let's go around back."

"Yes, we don't want the innkeeper to see us," said Mary.

"Why?" asked Luke

"Let's just say things got a little messy the last time we were here," said Peter.

One of the shepherds turned to Peter and Mary. "Here, hide behind us," he said.

Peter and Mary ducked behind the shepherds and walked past the inn. When they reached the stable, Peter saw donkeys, cows, and chickens—and two people leaning over a manger. A ray of

light from
the star shined
into the stable
and onto a baby
lying in the manger.

As they came closer,
the young lady turned.
Peter's eyes met hers. She
smiled. *I remember that smile,*
he thought. *I bumped into her
donkey when we were leaving the city!*

Peter also recognized the young man who had
been with the woman earlier that day. "Come in,"
the man said. "My name is Joseph."

"Angels sent us to see the baby who is to be the
Messiah and Savior," said one of the shepherds.

Joseph stepped aside and let the shepherds get
closer. They kneeled down and thanked God for
leading them to the promised King.

Peter, Mary, and Hank squeezed through the group of shepherds. Peter wanted to see the baby.

"His name is Jesus," said the young lady. "And my name is Mary."

"My name is Mary too," said Mary shyly. They smiled at each other.

Peter leaned closer to the manger. "Hi, Jesus," he whispered.

Peter thought he saw a little smile on Jesus' tiny face. A warm feeling filled Peter. There he was—God's only Son, the promised Savior, the Creator of the Universe, the Light of the World— sleeping in a manger right in front of Peter.

Michael was right, Peter thought. *The world would never be the same.*

7

THE KING IS BORN!

The shepherds shouted. "The Savior is born!"

Jesus opened his eyes, and Peter waited to see if he would cry. He didn't. He just blinked slowly and drifted back to sleep.

"Sorry about that," whispered one shepherd. "We're just excited."

The shepherds told Mary and Joseph about the angels and what they had said. Mary smiled, picked up her son, and held him in her arms.

Sunlight started to fill the stable, and Peter heard a rooster crow. Peter walked up by the side of the inn. People were beginning to come out of their homes and fill the streets.

"Let's tell everyone the good news!" said Luke.

The shepherds said goodbye to Joseph, Mary, and Jesus. They left the stable and ran down the dusty streets. They told everyone they met about Jesus—even some donkeys and chickens.

"The King is born!" shouted Luke.

"*Grrrr!*" Hank growled.

Peter turned around and saw the Commander stepping out of The King David Inn.

The Commander slipped his silver helmet on his head. "What's all the noise about?"

"The King is born," said Luke quietly.

The Commander stared down at Luke. "You already have a king!" he roared. "King Herod is your king—by order of the Great Roman Empire."

"But the new King has been born," said one of the shepherds.

"You don't get to decide who is king. Rome decides," snapped the Commander.

"No," said Peter. "God does!" He felt the adventure bag shake under his arm.

The Commander turned and looked straight at Peter. "What did you say?"

A shiver ran through Peter's body. He opened his mouth, but nothing came out.

Then the Commander turned back to Luke. "Where is this king?"

Luke looked at the Commander but didn't say anything.

"I don't trust you kids and your little secrets," said the Commander.

Peter could hear the shepherds in the distance telling the good news to more people in Bethlehem. He heard the people cheer.

"These people are out of control!" said the Commander. He turned and called to the other soldiers. "Remove these shepherds from Bethlehem! They are disturbing the peace!"

"Yes, Commander!" shouted the soldiers. "As you say!"

The soldiers drew their swords and headed toward the crowd.

The Commander turned back to Peter, Mary, and Luke. "I don't trust you three," he said. "I'll be watching you."

"*Grrrr.*" Hank growled at the Commander.

"You too," the Commander said to Hank. "Now get out of here! All of you!"

"Let's go!" said Peter.

They quickly left and made their way back out of Bethlehem. The shepherds joined them along the way.

As they walked through the city gate, Peter remembered something. "Hey, Luke," he said. "I need to talk to Mary for a second."

"Sure," said Luke. "I'll see you in a minute."

Hank ran ahead with Luke.

Mary looked at Peter. "What's wrong?"

"The scroll shook in the bag while we were talking to the Commander," he said.

"Maybe we solved one of the secret words," said Mary.

Peter pulled the scroll out of the bag and unrolled it. The first word on the scroll glowed and transformed into the word GOD.

"Yes!" said Peter. "We solved the first word."

"Now we only have three left," said Mary.

Suddenly, Peter heard horse hooves pounding behind him. He shoved the scroll in his bag and turned. The Commander was riding toward them on his tall white horse.

"I thought I told you to leave," he said.

"We are," said Peter. "We just stopped to rest."

The Commander narrowed his eyes and looked at them. Then he looked at the bag.

Peter grabbed Mary's hand and started walking backwards. "We'll be leaving now," said Peter. "Our friend is waiting for us."

"You better hurry," said the Commander. "And remember, I'll be watching you."

Peter and Mary turned and ran.

Before they caught up with the shepherds, Peter looked over his shoulder. "He's gone!"

Mary stopped and took some deep breaths. "I don't trust that guy," she said.

"Me either," said Peter. "It's almost like we've met him before."

"I was thinking the same thing," said Mary.

"Peter! Mary!" Luke called from up ahead. "Come on!"

"We're coming!" said Peter.

They joined the shepherds and traveled back to the valley.

Peter watched Hank chase sheep. He sighed. "It's a beautiful day."

As the sun began to set, Peter and Mary sat around a campfire with the shepherds and enjoyed bread and cheese for dinner. Peter listened as the shepherds talked about the angels and the new King.

"I can't believe God invited us to meet the King!" said one shepherd. "No one invites us to anything. Most people think we're dirty and smelly."

"I don't think you're smelly," said Peter. "But that stable sure was!" He pinched his nose.

The shepherds laughed. Everyone was so excited that it was hard to settle down. As the sky grew dark, the shepherds put out the campfire and wandered off to sleep.

Peter, Mary, and Hank climbed to the top of the hill and sat under an olive tree.

"Can you believe we met Jesus?" said Peter.

"I've seen drawings of baby Jesus," said Mary, "But seeing him in person? He was real—Jesus is real!"

"I can't wait to tell Mom and Dad!" said Peter. "I knew the stories they told us were true."

"I can't wait to tell Great-Uncle Solomon," said Mary. "Everything he's searched for is real!"

"It's amazing that God came to earth like that," said Peter, "as a tiny, little baby."

"He's so small and defenseless," said Mary.

"That's true," said Peter. "I hope Satan doesn't find Jesus and try to mess up God's plan."

"Me too," said Mary. "We need to figure out what Satan is up to so we can keep him from finding Jesus." She let out a big yawn. "But that will have to wait until tomorrow. I'm tired."

"I'm going to write down some things in my journal before I go to sleep," said Peter.

Mary rested her head under the olive tree. Hank curled up beside her. Peter took out his flashlight and his adventure journal and began to write.

Day 3

What an amazing day!
We got to meet baby Jesus!
I think he smiled at me.
Joseph and Mary were very
nice and took good care of
him. The shepherds were so excited that
the Great King is finally here. But I
don't trust the Commander. He didn't
seem happy about the news. That's all
for now. I'm so tired. I hope we get a
good night's sleep tonight.

Peter looked over at Mary and Hank. They
were already snoring. He closed his journal and
drifted off to sleep under the starry sky.

8

Do Sheep Swim?

Peter woke to Hank licking his face. "I'm awake, I'm awake!" He wiped Hank's slobber from his face and stretched.

"Good morning!" said Luke.

Peter looked up and saw Luke leaning against the olive tree.

Mary rubbed her eyes. "You're up early."

"A shepherd's day starts early," said Luke. "The sheep wake up with the sun."

"*Ruff!*" Hank barked and wagged his tail.

"Hank gets up early too," said Peter.

"I have a big day today, and I need your help," said Luke. "It's my turn to take some sheep to sell in Jerusalem."

"Why do you need help?" asked Mary.

Luke looked down and kicked a small stone. "I'm not a very good shepherd," he mumbled. "I need help keeping the sheep together."

Peter rolled up his sleeves. "I'll be glad to help," he said. "Do you have an extra shepherd's staff?"

"I was actually hoping Hank could help," said Luke. "But you and Mary can come too."

Peter felt a little embarrassed. "Oh yeah . . . I knew you were talking about Hank," he said. "Want to help with the sheep, Hank?"

"Woof!" Hank wagged his tail and ran in a circle.

"I think that's a yes," said Mary.

Luke smiled. "Let's go get the sheep."

Peter put the adventure bag over his shoulder,

and they headed down the hill. Sheep were everywhere. Luke looked around at each of the fluffy sheep.

"What are you looking for?" said Peter.

"I need to pick the perfect sheep," said Luke. "They can't have any spots or injuries."

"Why do they have to be perfect?" asked Mary.

"These lambs are going to be sacrificed at the Temple to help rescue us from our sins," said Luke. "To be a sacrifice, they have to be perfect."

"How's this one?" said Mary.

"Perfect!" said Luke.

Peter shook his head. Of course, Mary would be the first one to find a perfect sheep.

"I found one!" said Peter.

Luke looked carefully at the sheep. "Yes, it's perfect."

"Is it *more* perfect than Mary's?" asked Peter.

Mary rolled her eyes.
"You can't be more perfect
than perfect."

Luke nodded. "She's right."

Peter shrugged. "I thought I would give it a
shot."

After a while they finally had seven perfect
sheep. Luke packed some food for the road.

"Can I look at the map?" Mary asked Peter.

Peter shuffled through the bag. "Here it is."

Peter felt the scroll shake and jumped.
"Ahhh!"

"Is something wrong?" said Luke.

"No," said Peter. "I just need a minute with Mary."

"Okay," said Luke. "But we need to get going so we can get to Jerusalem before dark."

Peter and Mary ran over behind an olive tree. Peter pulled out the scroll and unrolled it. The second word on the scroll glowed and transformed into the word IS. Peter read, "God is _____ _____."

They gave each other a high-five.

"Is everything okay over there?" Luke said.

Peter shoved the scroll in the bag and handed the map to Mary. They walked back to Luke.

Mary pointed at the map. "It looks like we can take this road to Jerusalem," she said.

Luke looked at the map. "Where did you get that?"

"Our Great-Uncle gave it to us," said Peter. Mary gave him the "be careful" look.

"Oh," Luke said. "Well, that way is too long. I know a shortcut." Luke ran his finger along the path on the map. It was shorter, but it went across hills and valleys.

"Are you sure?" said Mary. "Wouldn't it be easier to go on the road?"

"It is. But the shortcut has more places for the sheep to eat and drink," said Luke.

Peter nodded. "Sounds good to me!"

"Follow me!" said Luke. He started walking straight ahead. None of the sheep moved.

"I'm not sure about this," Mary whispered to Peter.

Hank ran behind the sheep. *"Woof! Woof!"*

The sheep jumped up and started moving.

"It will be fine," said Peter. "Let's go."

They walked over hills—lots of hills. They walked through valleys—deep valleys. Peter was sweating and his feet were aching. He looked at

Mary. She was huffing and puffing too. Hank wasn't tired at all. He just kept running around the sheep, keeping them together.

"Can we take a little rest?" said Peter.

"We're almost there," said Luke. "Just two more hills."

They reached the top of the first hill. Peter looked down and saw a rushing river between them and the next hill. "Do sheep swim?"

"Of course, they do," said Mary, like everyone should know.

"That's true," said Luke. "But they really don't like doing it!"

Peter saw the sun beginning to set behind the last hill. "We need to hurry!"

They made their way down the hill to the edge of the rushing water. The sheep bleated, stuck their hooves in the muddy shore, and came to a standstill.

Luke hung his head. "We shouldn't have come this way. I'm always messing up."

"We have to keep going," said Mary. "We're almost there."

"We can do it," said Peter. "Trust God and keep going!"

"You're right," said Luke. "God will help me." He jumped into the rushing water and swam across. He stood up on the other side and shouted for the sheep.

The sheep didn't move. Then Hank started barking behind them and they leapt into the water. Peter watched them

swim across. They looked like white, puffy clouds floating across the river.

"They're swimming!" said Peter.

"I told you they could swim," said Mary. She jumped in after them and swam across.

Peter jumped in with the adventure bag. He swam a little slower than the sheep. The water started moving faster, and Peter got pulled under. He struggled to the surface and took a breath. He saw everyone waiting for him on the riverbank.

"Hurry!" shouted Mary. "The water is getting rougher."

"I know!" sputtered Peter. He held the bag tightly under one arm and swam with the other. Finally, he made it to the other side.

He climbed up the shore and took a deep breath. "Did all of the sheep make it across?"

Luke quickly counted them. "There are only six. One is missing!"

9

CAMELS IN THE COURTYARD

Baaaa!

Peter turned and saw the last sheep rushing down the river. The lamb's head went under the crashing water.

Luke threw down his staff, ran to the river, and dove in. He grabbed the sheep and swam to the shore.

He carried the soggy sheep out of the water. The other sheep nuzzled the wet one. Luke walked back over to Peter, Mary, and Hank.

"See?" said Peter. "You *are* a good shepherd."

Luke smiled. "I guess I am. Now let's go!"

Everyone, including the sheep, followed Luke up the last hill.

Luke stopped at the top and held up his arm. "Welcome to Jerusalem!"

"It's beautiful!" said Mary.

"See that building there?" Luke pointed at the tall white building that Peter had seen through his telescope. "That's the Temple."

"It's even bigger than I thought it would be," said Peter. He saw a tall stone wall around the outside of the city. There were mighty towers, a massive palace, and houses everywhere— some big and others small.

The sky grew darker as the sun set behind the golden roof of the Temple.

"Let's get inside the gate before it's too dark," said Luke.

They made their way down a path on the side of the hill. They found stone steps leading to a small gate in the wall.

"This is the Sheep Gate," said Luke. "We can enter here."

They walked through the gate and found a large area filled with shepherds and sheep.

Mary plopped down on the ground and rubbed her ankle.

"Are you okay?" asked Luke.

"Yeah," said Mary. "I'm just a little tired from the long walk."

Peter yawned. "Me too."

Luke pointed to an open spot beside the Temple. "We can sleep over there."

Hank and the sheep nestled down on top of some straw. Peter rested his head on the adventure bag and drifted off to sleep.

Baaaa! Baaaa! The sound of sheep and the bustle of shepherds woke Peter up.

"Let's hurry!" said Luke. "We need to get a good spot at the Temple to sell the sheep."

They jumped up from the straw and gathered the sheep. Peter and Mary followed Luke up some steps and stepped into a beautiful courtyard. The ground was covered in white marble and tall columns surrounded them.

In the middle of the courtyard, Peter saw the Temple. He looked up at the beautiful building. The sound of trumpets filled the air.

Luke pointed to a spot between two columns. "There's a good spot," he said.

Peter watched as people flooded into the courtyard from every direction. Then he noticed men riding tall camels. They wore purple robes with golden stars stitched around the edges.

Peter thought they looked like kings. Everyone gathered around them—including several men dressed in white from head to toe.

Peter pointed. "Who are those men in white?" he asked Luke.

"They're priests," Luke replied.

Peter heard two of the priests talking. "What are Magi doing at the Temple?" said one.

"I don't know," said the other.

One of the priests stepped forward and greeted the Magi. "Welcome," he said. "What brings you to the Temple?"

"We have followed a star on a long journey through the desert and across many hills to see the newborn King of the Jews," said one of the Magi. "We have come to worship him and bring him gifts."

Peter felt the excitement build in the crowd around him.

"The King is born!" shouted a man.

An older lady clapped her hands. "The Messiah has finally come to rescue us!"

"Where is this new King?" asked an old man with a long white beard.

"The star we were following disappeared," said the first Magi. "We stopped here hoping someone would know where to find the child."

"Oh no!" Mary pointed. "Look who it is."

Peter turned and saw the Commander riding in on his white horse.

"Silence!" the Commander bellowed. His voice echoed off the Temple walls.

The crowd quieted.

"What's all this noise about?" he said.

"The King of the Jews has been born," said the man with the long white beard.

The Commander pulled the horse's reins and trotted over to the old man. "There isn't a new king!" he shouted. "King Herod is the King of

the Jews." He pulled out his sword and thrust it in the air.

The crowd grumbled. Peter could tell they did not like King Herod or the Commander.

The Commander rode over to the priests. "Who caused this disturbance of the peace?"

One of the priests pointed at the Magi. "They did!" he said. "We tried to keep them quiet."

The Commander approached the Magi. "So, you're the ones spreading this lie about a new king," he said.

"It's not a lie," said one of the Magi. "The promised King has come. We saw his star."

"I'm sure King Herod would like to find out more about this star and new king," said the Commander. "Come with me!"

Peter and Mary froze. The Commander was coming straight toward them.

10

A Secret Plot

The Commander stopped his horse in front of Peter and Mary.

"You kids seem to show up wherever there's trouble," he said. "Stay here. I'll be back for you."

Peter pinched his nose as the camels walked past. "They *have* been on a long journey."

As the Commander led the Magi out of the courtyard, Peter said, "Let's follow them."

Mary wrinkled her forehead. "I don't know," she said. "What if the Commander sees us?"

"We'll stay back so he can't," said Peter. "But

the Magi might need our help to find Jesus."

Peter leaned in close to Mary and whispered so Luke couldn't hear. "Maybe they'll lead us to a clue that helps us solve the scroll."

Mary nodded.

"You sure have a lot of secrets," said Luke.

"It's complicated," said Mary.

"We're going to follow the Magi," said Peter. "Do you want to come with us?"

"I can't," said Luke. "I need to stay and take care of the sheep."

"You really are a good shepherd," said Peter.

"Thank you," said Luke. "I hope I see you both again."

"I hope so," said Peter.

"Goodbye," said Mary. She gave Luke a hug.

Luke bent down to pet Hank on the head.

"Let's go, Hank," said Peter. "Before the Magi get too far ahead of us."

They left the Temple. Mary shaded her eyes from the sun as she looked down the stone-covered street. "I don't see them," she said.

"Those are some fast camels," said Peter. "Where do you think they went?"

Hank put his nose in the air and sniffed. *"Woof!"*

"Do you smell the camels, Hank?" said Mary.

"That wouldn't be too hard," Peter said. "I think *I* still smell them. Find those camels, Hank!"

Hank took off like a lightning bolt. Peter and Mary ran behind him as fast as they could, darting and dodging through crowded streets. They ran past a stadium packed with people cheering for a chariot race.

Peter huffed and puffed as he ran. "I wish we had a chariot like we did in Babylon," he said. "This would be much easier."

They ran through a long line of people waiting

to enter a huge outdoor theater surrounded by tall pillars.

"Sorry!" said Peter. "Enjoy the show!"

Hank took a sharp right turn and headed down a street lined with houses. The houses got bigger and bigger as they ran down the street.

"We must be in the nice part of town," said Peter.

Hank led them through an arched gate in a wall. The camels and the Commander's horse stood in front of an amazing palace.

Mary bent over to catch her breath. "Where are the Magi?" she panted.

Peter wiped sweat from his forehead and looked at the front of the palace. "I don't see them anywhere."

"They must be inside," said Mary.

Peter pointed at the guards at the palace entrance. "How are we going to get in?"

"*Ruff!*" Hank ran around the side of the palace.

Peter and Mary followed and found Hank scratching at a door.

Peter looked around. He didn't see any guards. "Let's see if it's locked." He reached for the handle and pulled. The door slowly creaked open. Peter stepped into a long hallway. Mary held the door open for Hank, then closed it behind them.

"Stay behind us, Hank," whispered Mary.

Peter felt the adventure bag shake. He tapped Mary on the shoulder. "The scroll shook," he whispered.

Mary looked down the hall. "The coast looks clear," she said.

Peter pulled out the scroll and unrolled it. The fourth word glowed and transformed into the word US.

Mary read, "God is _____ us."

"We have one word left and only two days to

solve the secret of the scroll," said Peter.

"We'll figure it out," said Mary. "Now let's go find the Magi."

They quietly crept down the hallway. Peter could hear people talking as they neared the door at the end of the hall. He peeked through the doorway and saw a huge room with tall pillars around the edges. Colorful rugs covered the floor. The Magi stood in the middle of the room facing a large throne.

"Let's get closer so we can hear what they're saying," whispered Peter.

They crawled behind the huge pillars until they reached a large pot on the side of the room. Peter peeked around the pot. A man sat on the throne wearing a red robe and a gold crown.

That must be King Herod, Peter thought. The Commander stood beside the throne, and a priest stood behind it.

"So, you are looking for the King of the Jews?" asked King Herod.

"Yes," said one of the Magi. "We saw his star and have come to worship him."

King Herod stood up. "Well, here I am."

"It is an honor to meet you," said another Magi. "But we are searching for the newborn King."

"I'm not sure what you mean," said King Herod. "My firstborn son is no longer a child."

"We are looking for the Great King," said another Magi. "The Messiah that was written about by the Jewish prophets."

Peter saw King Herod's face turn red with anger. The Commander whispered something in the king's ear.

King Herod took a deep breath and tried to smile. "Where does the prophecy say this king will be born?"

"Pardon me, your majesty!" The priest walked out from behind the throne. "I have the prophecy here on this scroll."

King Herod turned to the priest. "Well, read it for everyone to hear."

The priest unrolled the scroll and read, "But you, Bethlehem, in the land of Judah, are not the least important. For a ruler will come from you who will be the Shepherd of my people, Israel."

The Commander whispered to the king.

The king nodded. "Everyone leave!" he ordered. "I want to speak to the Magi in private."

Everyone left the room except for the Magi, King Herod, and the Commander.

"Should we leave?" whispered Mary.

Peter shook his head and sat very still. He listened closely to the king's conversation.

"When did you see this star?" asked the king.

"Many days ago," said one of the Magi. "We have come on a long journey."

"I would like for you to go and find this newborn king," said King Herod. "Then come back and let me know where he is so I can go and worship him too."

"Yes. Of course, your majesty!" said a Magi. "We will return after we find him."

Peter watched the Magi leave the room. Mary started to move, but Peter stopped her. Something told him they should stay.

"All right," said King Herod. "Why did you have me ask the Magi to return with this pretend king's location?"

"Because if you can find him," snarled the Commander, "you can destroy him."

"*Grrrr.*" Hank made a low growl.

"What was that?" said King Herod. "Is someone there?"

Peter crouched down lower as he heard footsteps coming toward them.

11

FOLLOW THAT STAR!

Peter's heart pounded so loudly that he was sure the Commander would hear it. The footsteps sounded closer and closer.

"Run!" shouted Peter.

They jumped to their feet and ran for the door as fast as their feet and paws could carry them. Peter swung the door open, and they ran down the hallway. He looked over his shoulder. The Commander was close on their heels.

Between breaths, Peter yelled, "Michael! Help!"

Huffing and puffing, Peter yanked the palace

door open, and they sprinted outside. The door slammed behind them. Peter turned, expecting to see the Commander. But it was Michael, holding the door shut with his flaming sword in his hand.

"I'll hold him for a while," said Michael. "Go and find the Magi. You must warn them not to tell King Herod where Jesus is."

Bang! The door shook behind Michael.

"Hurry!" said Michael.

Peter, Mary, and Hank ran from the palace.

"Hank, find the Magi!" said Peter.

Hank sniffed the air and took off running. He led them back to the city's edge and through a gate in the city's wall.

Peter stopped and looked out at the road. "There they are!" He took off running again.

Mary and Hank caught up just as Peter stopped before the Magi.

"Are you searching for the newborn King?" asked Peter.

"Yes," said a Magi. "How did you know?"

"We heard you talking about him at the Temple," said Mary.

The Magi's shoulders slumped. "Yes, we are not sure where to go," he said. "We can't see the star we were following anymore. I'm not sure we'll ever find the newborn King."

"We can help! We've seen him!" said Peter.

"Where?" asked another Magi.

"In a stable in Bethlehem," said Mary.

The first Magi clapped his hands. "It's true!" He turned to the other Magi. "The prophecies are true."

The second Magi shook his head. "He may already be gone."

"Why?" asked Peter.

"Because his star is gone," said the Magi.

"You can't stop searching now," said Peter. "You're so close."

"He's right," said a Magi. "We must go to Bethlehem at once."

Peter looked at the sun beginning to set behind Jerusalem. "We need to hurry!"

One of the Magi pulled a map out of a bag hanging on the side of his camel. "Bethlehem is down this road," he said, pointing at the map.

Peter's heart skipped a beat. The Magi's map looked just like the map Great-Uncle Solomon gave Mary. He nudged Mary and pointed. "That looks just like your map."

Mary's eyes got really big. "It does," she whispered. "But it's not missing the top corner."

"True," said Peter. "Maybe it's not the same."

Just then, a camel leaned over and took a bite out of the map.

"Bad camel!" said the Magi. He rolled up the map and put it back in the bag.

The camel made a sour face, curled his lips, and spit the piece of map straight at Peter.

"Watch out!" said Mary.

Peter tried to duck, but the slobbery ball of paper hit him in the forehead.

"Woof!" Hank ran over and picked it up.

"Gross!" said Peter. "Put that down."

Hank dropped it.

"No, save it," said Mary. "It could be the missing piece to my map."

"Yuck!" said Peter.

97

He picked up the paper and slung off some of the slobber before putting it in the adventure bag.

"Let's go see the King!" said Peter.

The Magi rode their camels as Peter, Mary, and Hank walked along the gravel road. The sky grew darker and darker.

"This is farther than I remember," said Peter.

"We need to rest," said the second Magi.

The camels bent their long legs and sat on the ground. Peter and Mary helped the Magi set up their tents on the side of the road. They even had an extra one for Peter and Mary. Hank stayed outside with the camels.

"Good night," said the Magi. "We'll continue our journey in the morning."

Peter rested his head on the adventure bag and fell asleep. After what felt like only a few hours, he felt Hank tugging on his sleeve. Peter rubbed his eyes and looked out of the tent. It was still dark.

"*Ruff!*" Hank ran out of the tent. Peter got up and followed him. Then Hank howled at something in the night sky.

Peter yawned. "What is it?"

He got his telescope and looked into the dark sky. He saw the moon and the stars, then a super bright star caught his attention. There it was— right over Bethlehem.

Mary and the Magi wandered out of their tents. "There's the star!" Peter said, pointing above Bethlehem.

"It's back!" said a Magi. "The star is back!"

Everyone quickly packed up the camp. "We need to go now," said another Magi, "while we can still see the star!"

After packing up the camels, the Magi continued their journey through the cool night air. They followed the light of the star. Peter, Mary, and Hank followed them.

Finally, they made it to Bethlehem. Peter led the way down the dark, quiet streets toward the stable.

"This way," said Peter. "We're almost there."

They walked to The King David Inn, but the star wasn't there.

Peter started to get a little worried. He led the Magi around the inn to the stable, but the star wasn't there either. He ran inside. Joseph, Mary, and Jesus were gone!

12

GIFTS FOR A KING

Peter's shoulders sagged as he walked out of the stable. "I thought they would be here."

"We need to follow the star more closely," said a Magi.

They looked into the sky. It was getting lighter by the minute as the sun began to rise.

"It's getting too light," said Peter.

"Keep looking!" said the Magi. "We still have a little time."

"There it is!" Mary pointed toward the outskirts of town.

Peter could just see the star hovering in the sky. They followed and made their way to a small house on the edge of Bethlehem as quickly as they could. Just as they arrived, the star disappeared into the light of day.

Peter nudged Mary. "This looks like the house King David grew up in."

"You're right," said Mary.

Hank ran up and scratched at the door. Then one of the Magi knocked.

The door swung open. Joseph stood in the doorway.

"We have come on a long journey to see the baby who will be King of the Jews," said a Magi.

"Come in," said Joseph.

Peter peeked around the Magi. There was Jesus, resting in his mother's arms. The Magi fell to their knees in front of Jesus. They pulled out their gifts to present to the newborn.

The first Magi opened his box. "Gold," he said. "A gift for a king."

Next, the second Magi opened his box. "Frankincense," he said. "A gift for a priest."

The third Magi opened his box. "Myrrh," he said. "An ointment for healing. May this child bring healing to the nations."

Mary smiled as she cradled Jesus in her arms. "Thank you," she said. Then she saw Peter, Mary, and Hank standing behind the men. "It's good to see you again."

Joseph turned to the Magi. "Are you staying in Bethlehem tonight?"

"We hope to. We must give the camels a rest before we start our journey," said the first Magi. "Maybe we can stay at The King David Inn. The stable looked perfect for the camels."

"It's okay," said Peter. *If you don't mind the smell*, he thought.

Joseph looked at Peter and Mary. "It looks like you need to rest as well," he said. "Where will you stay?"

Peter looked at Mary. "I don't know . . ."

"You can stay here," said Joseph. "There's plenty of room."

"Thank you," said Mary.

"This will be much better than the stable," said Peter.

"It is," said Joseph. "Believe me. It is."

Mary stood up with Jesus in her arms. "Please stay for breakfast. Joseph and I would love to hear about your travels."

Everyone ate a breakfast of bread, fruit, and olives. The Magi talked about their journey following the star across the desert. Hank stayed close to Jesus as the baby slept. Peter and Mary helped clean up as Joseph helped the Magi load up the camels.

"Goodbye," said Peter as the Magi climbed on their camels.

"Thank you for your help," said the men. Then the camels slowly began their walk down the dusty street toward the inn.

Peter and Mary went back inside the house. They spent the afternoon with Joseph and Mary and baby Jesus. Peter went with Joseph to the Bethlehem market to buy food for dinner. At the end of the day, Joseph showed Peter, Mary, and Hank to their room. "You can sleep in here."

"Thank you," said Peter.

Mary walked up with Jesus in her arms. "I

hope Jesus doesn't keep you up tonight," she said. "We'll see you in the morning."

Peter closed the door and laid the adventure bag on a small table.

"Can you believe that we just spent an entire day with Jesus, Mary, and Joseph?" Mary asked.

"It's amazing!" said Peter. "We're sleeping in the same house as Jesus!"

"I know! But now we need to focus on solving the secret in the scroll," said Mary. "We only have one day left."

"I almost forgot," said Peter. He took the scroll out of the bag and handed it to Mary.

She unrolled it on the floor. "God is _____ us," she read.

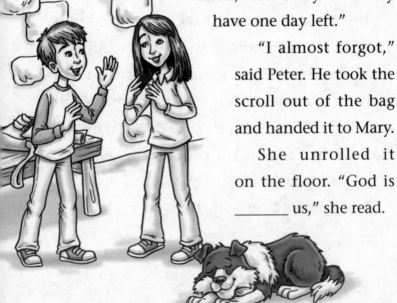

Peter scratched his head. "I got it," he said. "God is for us."

Nothing happened to the scroll.

"God is helping us," said Mary.

Nothing happened to the scroll.

Peter snapped his fingers. "This has to be it," he said. "God is near us."

Nothing happened to the scroll.

Peter sighed. "I thought that would be it," he said. "He is in the same house."

"That's true," said Mary. "It was a good guess."

They tried and tried but couldn't solve the secret.

Mary yawned and rolled up the scroll. "I guess we'll try again tomorrow." She lay down on a mat and drifted off to sleep. Hank curled up by the door and started snoring. Peter took out his adventure journal and sat by the window to write by the light of the star.

Day 6

It has been a great adventure. I can't believe we got to meet Jesus, Mary, and Joseph! It was nice of them to let us stay with them. I hope the Magi have a safe journey home. Oh no! I forgot to warn them not to tell King Herod where Jesus is. I don't trust Herod or the Commander. I will have to trust God.

"Grrrr!"

Peter put the journal down and looked over at Hank. He was growling at the door. Then someone knocked.

Mary jumped out of bed. "What's happening?"

Peter opened the door. It was Joseph, and he looked worried. Mary stood behind him, holding Jesus.

"What's wrong?" asked Peter.

"An angel appeared in my dream and gave me a message!" said Joseph.

"What did he say?" asked Peter.

"He told me to get up and escape to Egypt with Jesus and Mary," said Joseph.

"Why?" said Peter.

"The angel said that King Herod is going to try to kill Jesus," said Joseph.

Peter shook his head. "I knew we couldn't trust King Herod or the Commander."

Mary looked at Peter, then back at Joseph. "When will you leave?"

"As soon as we can pack up," said Joseph.

"We can help!" said Peter.

Under the dark of night, they gathered food

and water and the gifts from the Magi and loaded them on the donkey.

Joseph helped Mary onto the donkey and handed Jesus to her.

"Thank you for your help," said Joseph. "You are welcome to stay in this house until you return to your home, wherever that may be."

Mary held Jesus close and smiled at them. "Maybe we'll see you again one day."

"I hope so," said Peter.

Peter and Mary waved as they left.

Peter tried to sleep, but he tossed and turned and worried. What if they couldn't solve the secret of the scroll? What if Joseph, Mary, and Jesus didn't make it to Egypt before the Commander found them?

Peter prayed, "Dear God, please help us." He closed his eyes and finally slept.

13

IN THE NICK OF TIME

A rooster crowed and woke Peter. He shook Mary's shoulder. "Wake up!"

Mary yawned. "I'm so tired," she said. "Just let me sleep a little longer."

"We can sleep later," said Peter. "I remembered that Michael said to warn the Magi not to tell King Herod where Jesus is."

"We can't," said Mary. "We need to solve the scroll today or we will be stuck here."

"We need to tell the Magi first," said Peter. "Joseph, Mary, and Jesus need time to escape."

"Okay," said Mary. "But let's hurry."

Peter grabbed the adventure bag, and they headed out with Hank to find the Magi.

"Where do you think they are?" asked Mary.

"I think they said they were going to stay at The King David Inn," said Peter.

Mary frowned. "I hope the innkeeper doesn't see us."

"We'll just have to be careful," said Peter.

They made their way through the little town of Bethlehem. It was so early that the streets were almost empty. They rounded the corner and found the inn. The front door was open. Peter crouched down and slowly peeked inside. The innkeeper was asleep behind his desk.

"The coast is clear," he whispered.

They tiptoed past the innkeeper to look for the Magi. They knocked on every door in the inn, but the Magi weren't in any of the rooms.

They went to the stable to see if the camels were there. They weren't.

Peter saw a young girl sweeping in the stable.

"Have you seen men dressed in purple robes with camels around here?" asked Peter.

"They're gone," said the girl.

"Do you know where they went?" asked Mary.

"I don't know," said the girl. "They left in a hurry a few hours ago. They said something about an angel in a dream."

"Thanks for your help," said Mary.

The young girl went back to sweeping.

"Grrrr!" Peter turned to see what Hank was growling at just as the Commander came riding up on his white horse.

"Well, look who we have here," he said. "The little troublemakers and their nasty little dog."

"Grrrr!" Hank crouched down low.

"Where are your soldiers?" said Peter.

"I don't need any help," the Commander said. "I'm on a little spy mission. Those Magi didn't return to King Herod, so I've come to look for the new king myself."

The Commander hopped off his horse and walked toward them. "Where is he?" he said. "I know you've seen him."

"We won't tell!" said Peter.

The Commander pulled out his sword.

"Where is he?" he shouted. He walked past Peter and Mary and looked into the stable.

The young girl screamed and ran out.

The Commander stomped back over to Peter, Mary, and Hank.

"He's not here," said Peter. "And you will never find him."

"You think some kids and a little dog can stop my plan?" said the Commander. "If I don't find him, King Herod and his soldiers will!"

"We may not be able to stop you," said Peter. "But God can."

"By sending Michael?" said the Commander.

"You know about Michael?" Peter asked.

"I've battled Michael for many, many years," said the Commander.

Peter looked into the Commander's eyes and realized that he was Satan, the enemy.

"We should have known it was you, Satan," said Mary.

"Yes, it took you quite a while to figure it out," said the Commander.

"You won't win," said Peter.

"God won't stop me," said the Commander. "He's far, far away in heaven. He doesn't care about this world."

"Yes, he does," said Peter. "God loves the world so much that He sent his own Son to be with us and rescue us." Peter felt the scroll shaking in his bag. He quickly pulled it out and unrolled it.

"Peter, look!" said Mary. The third word on the scroll glowed and transformed into the word WITH.

"You aren't going to get away this time!" said the Commander. He pulled out his long, sharp sword and moved toward them.

Mary quickly read the scroll, "GOD IS WITH US!"

Suddenly, the ground started shaking. Hank started barking. Then everything started to spin.

When the spinning stopped, Peter and Mary stood safely in the middle of Great-Uncle Solomon's library. Everything was just as they left it. The scroll's red wax seal transformed into a medallion with a star on it.

Great-Uncle Solomon opened the library door. "You're back! How was your adventure?"

"It was amazing," said Mary. "We saw Jesus!"

"Tell me everything!" said Great-Uncle Solomon.

Peter told Great-Uncle Solomon about escaping the hyenas on the way to Bethlehem. Mary told him about sleeping in the stable and the mean innkeeper. Peter told him about Luke and the shepherds. He told how the telescope helped them find the star and how they met Joseph, Mary, and Jesus. Then Mary told

Great-Uncle Solomon about the Magi and the map.

"Oh yeah," said Peter. "I almost forgot." He reached into his bag. He pulled out Mary's map and the crumpled up corner of the Magi's map that the camel had spit at him. He flattened out the piece as Mary unrolled the map. Then he placed the piece where the missing corner of Mary's map should be.

Great-Uncle Solomon leaped into the air. "It's a perfect fit!" he said, clapping his hands.

"You were right," said Mary. "It really is the Magi's map!"

"Yes, it is!" said Great-Uncle Solomon. "Be very careful with that map. It is quite a treasure."

"I will," said Mary.

"What about King Herod and the soldiers?" asked Peter. "I'm worried that they might have found Jesus."

Great-Uncle Solomon
pulled his red Bible from
the shelf and sat down
in his big leather chair.
"Let me tell you the rest
of the story."

He told them that the Magi
were warned by an angel not to tell King Herod
where Jesus was. He told them that Joseph, Mary,
and Jesus made it safely to Egypt, then went back
to Israel after King Herod died.

"What happened next?" said Peter.

Great-Uncle Solomon closed his Bible. "That
is an adventure for another day," he said.

Peter looked at the medallion of the star in his
hand. He couldn't wait for their next adventure.

Do you want to read more about the events in this story?

The people, places, and events in *The King Is Born* are drawn from the stories in the Bible. You can read more about them in the following passages in the Bible.

Luke 2:1–7 tells the story of Mary and Joseph traveling to Bethlehem for the birth of Jesus.

Luke 2:8–20 tells about the angels announcing the birth of Jesus to the shepherds.

Matthew 2:1–12 tells about the Magi following the star to Jerusalem, meeting King Herod, and visiting Jesus.

Matthew 2:13–23 tells the story of Joseph, Mary, and Jesus escaping to Egypt because King Herod sent his soldiers to kill all the boys under two years old in Bethlehem.

Special Notes:

1. Luke is a fictional character representing the Jewish children living in Israel during the birth of Jesus.

2. Events in *The King Is Born* have been condensed. The visit of the Magi could have taken place up to two years after the birth of Jesus.

CATCH ALL
PETER AND MARY'S ADVENTURES!

In *The Beginning*, Peter, Mary, and Hank witness the Creation of the earth while battling a sneaky snake.

In *Race to the Ark*, the trio must rush to help Noah finish the ark before the coming flood.

In *The Great Escape*, Peter, Mary, and Hank journey to Egypt and see the devastation of the plagues.

In *Journey to Jericho*, the trio lands in Jericho as the Israelites prepare to enter the Promised Land.

In ***The Shepherd's Stone***, Peter, Mary, and Hank accompany David as he prepares to fight Goliath.

In ***The Lion's Roar***, the trio arrive in Babylon and uncover a secret plot to get Daniel thrown in the lions' den.

In ***The King Is Born***, Peter, Mary, and Hank visit Bethlehem at the time of Jesus' birth.

In ***Miracles by the Sea***, the trio meets Jesus and the disciples and witnesses amazing miracles.

In ***The Final Scroll***, Peter, Mary, and Hank travel back to Jerusalem and witness Jesus' crucifixion and resurrection.

ABOUT THE AUTHOR

Mike Thomas grew up in Florida playing sports and riding his bike to the library and the arcade. He graduated from Liberty University, where he earned a bachelor's degree in Bible Studies.

When his son Peter was nine years old, Mike went searching for books that would teach Peter about the Bible in a fun and imaginative way. Finding none, he decided to write his own series. In The Secret of the Hidden Scrolls, Mike combines biblical accuracy with adventure, imagination, and characters who are dear to his heart. The main characters are named after Mike's son Peter, his niece Mary, and his dog, Hank.

Mike Thomas lives in Tennessee with his wife, Lori; two sons, Payton and Peter; and Hank.

For more information about the author and the series, visit www.secretofthehiddenscrolls.com.